tuned in

EPISODE #8

movie
madness

by Julia DeVillers

Printed in the United States of America

First edition

ISBN 0-9752713-1-8

Visit www.limitedtoo.com

introduction

This Journal Belongs to: ☆

Maddy Elizabeth Sparks

☆   Private! Keep Out!!!   ☆

You know who you are!!! ZACK!!!

OK! I've got a problem! I've got to make up my mind about something! See, here's the deal.

Tomorrow is school picture day. And ...

What do I wear? I have no clue. I need the perfect outfit this year.

Because last year, I was more like, whatever. I mean I took some time picking out my shirt. Because even if it's just your face, you can see a little of your shirt peeking out.

I wore a cool choker. Had a decent hair day. So it should have been fine, right?

But then ... I made a major mistake.

Because they did something new. Before it was always that headshot! Just your face! Just a little bit of your shirt!

But last year they took a class picture, too. With our whole bodies in it. I was in the front row. I was standing next to Taylor. Taylor! My BFF even though she moved! She looked cute! And fun! Like always. On the other side of me was Brittany. She was totally fashion. Totally stylin. Like always.

Then there was me. My top half was pretty OK!

But I didn't know my whole body was going to be in a picture! And my pants so didn't match right. My outfit was ... ugh! Total yikes!

But this year I have a plan! I will wear the perfect outfit!

Because a picture in a yearbook? Everyone sees that! So this year I need to look good.

So everyone in my school will have a picture of me, Maddy Sparks, saved forever! Looking good! For a change!

So ... **PRESSURE!!!!** What am I going to wear???!!!!

I was on the bus ride home. I had to hide my journal with my hand.

Because I sit next to Brittany. And sometimes I think she peeks at what I'm writing.

Brittany's my ex-friend. We used to be friends! But then she got ... mean! And nasty! And then it was like ...

Boom!

She wasn't my friend anymore.

But I still had to sit next to her on the bus. Assigned seats. No switching.

Brittany was talking to Haley across the aisle.

"Soooo Hay, what did you decide for yearbook pictures?" Brittany was asking. "The first outfit or the second?"

"I think the second?" Haley said back. "Unless you like the first better?"

"Better make the right choice," Brittany warned. "You'll be standing next to me. Gotta represent."

"Uh ... which one do you like best?" Haley asked her.

"Oh, it's so obvious," Brittany said. "I'm sure you'll pick the right one."

"Well, what are YOU wearing, Brittany?" Haley asked her.

I listened. Because Brittany? Always seemed to know the right styles. Maybe I could match what she was wearing.

"Secret," Brittany said. "Totally confidential. Don't copy me. No posers allowed."

Or not.

"But it's totally hype. Mom took me for some major mall-age last night. Major maxing out of my plastic," Brittany said.

"That's a credit card, for those of you who do not have their own," Brittany added. "So, speaking of people who don't have their own plastic ... Maddy! What are you wearing for yearbook pictures?"

Uh oh. Brittany doesn't talk to me too much. And when she does? Usually not good.

"Um ... I don't know yet." I said.

"Really? I'm surprised that after last year's fashion disaster you haven't been worrying about it," Brittany said, cheerfully. "I mean puh-lease! Flowered shirt with those blue pants? So wrong."

Brittany kept talking. Blah blah blah, stress stress stress.

"You do realize your yearbook picture is very important. I mean, everyone sees it. Forever! I mean, my Mom still has her yearbook. So even like a gajillion years later people see it. People will remember your outfit choice forever and ever."

OK. One thing. I know this is not the world's most important problem. I know this is not like world peace or something. It's just a silly picture.

OK, but a silly picture that is very important to me!!!! So yes! This year! I will wear the RIGHT outfit for the yearbook picture!

Except, I don't know what "right" is.

AUGH!!!!

The bus pulled up to my street. It was my turn to get off.

"Wait til you see my outfit!" Brittany was saying. "Total movie star!"

OK. I'm so getting off this bus. I walked home. OK. I needed a plan. I needed to get to the mall. Tonight! To buy something latest and greatest.

Or at least good enough for yearbook!

chapter 1

I walked in my front door.

I needed some cheering up. I knew just what would do it!

Mwah! Mwah! I made little kissy noises. I heard little tiny footsteps coming and there was ...

BUGGIE!

My sweet little Lovebug! My white fluffy puppy!

I picked her up and she licked my nose.

"Hi cute little Buggie," I said. I gave her some hugs.

I looove having a dog!!! Buggie nuzzled up against me.

I went into the kitchen.

"I'm home!" I yelled. "Mooom?!"

I needed to talk to Mom. Right away! This is what I'm thinking. I tell my Mom the importance of a new outfit for yearbook. And tada! We're off to the mall.

"Hah-cha!"

ACK!

My brother Zack jumped out from the stairs. Totally freaked me out!

I looove having a dog! I don't always looove having a brother.

"Chawa ... HA! Hay-ah! Cha!" Zack was jumping around doing karate kick things at me.

"Zack!" I said, holding Buggie close. "Watch out for Buggie! Stop it."

Zack bowed.

"I am Master Zack," he said.

"Can Master Zack tell me where his mother is?" I asked.

"Five bucks," Zack said. "Five bucks for that information."

"Remember what Mom and Dad said," I said. "No bribing me! Just tell me where they are."

"Alrighty," Zack said. "But first ... check this out."

Zack spun around. He pointed to his uniform.

"Nice threads, eh?" he said. "I'm taking tae kwan do lessons."

He spun around and kicked and chopped at me. With more hah-chas.

Oh, great. Now my brother's going to be chopping and kicking. My parents OK'd this?

"Nice outfit," I said. "Now where's Mom?"

So hopefully ... I can get a new outfit, too!

Zack bowed to me.

"Thank you for the kind words. Your esteemed mother is in the basement," Zack said. "See? Whatcha think? Don't I sound like a real tae kwan do dude?"

"Um, sure," I told him.

I ran downstairs.

"How was your day?" my Mom asked. She was scrapbooking.

"OK," I said. "But yearbook pictures are tomorrow! And I have nothing to wear! So can we go to the mall please?"

"Honey, not tonight. I have my scrapbook group coming over."

"Please please please! I need something perfect for pictures!" I told her. "Everyone sees your yearbook picture. Forever!"

"In fact," Mom said. "I just made a new page in my scrapbook. It's so sweet!"

She showed me a scrapbook page with pictures of me from last year. One of the pictures was – ugh! That group photo.

"I photocopied it from your yearbook," Mom said. "That way we'll have it in your scrapbook, too. To remember forever."

OK! Could we be taking a little mall trip then!

"But that's part of the fun," my Mom was still talking. "Looking back at your old yearbooks and laughing at your pictures. Remember that photo of me from high school with the big hair? I made my hair that tall on purpose! That was the fashion! What were we thinking?"

She was laughing.

I was not!

"And the frosty blue eye shadow?" she was still laughing.

"Mooooom!" I said. "That was then! This is now!"

"Anyway," she said. "Shopping sounds fun. Let's go Saturday."

Saturday?! That's too late!

It was hopeless!

"Hah-cha!" we heard Zack yell. "Hey, guys! Come upstairs and see my new move. Spin-kick-punch and Chawa-HA!"

"Let's go humor him," Mom said, heading upstairs. "Get it out of his system before my scrapbook group comes."

"Why are you letting Zack take those classes?" I asked. "Now he's all kicking and chopping at me."

"The brochure says it is supposed to teach self-control," Mom said. "So the kicking and chopping at family members should stop after he takes a lesson. That's what I'm hoping anyway."

I hope so.

But now ... I have other issues.

No mall! No shopping! No major "maxing of plastic"! No minor handing over of cash, even!

That means I have to find the right yearbook outfit. In my own closet!

Help!

chapter 2

Maddy's Yearbook Outfit Choices:

★ Blue shirt with the flare-y skirt???
★ Ruffly shirt with denim scooter???
★ Black shirt with pants with patches on them???

OK. Not bad, actually. I had narrowed it down to three choices. I laid out all my outfits on my bed. Which one would look best?

I need a fashion consultant.

"Buggie, which one do you like? Sniff one." I told her.

Buggie jumped off the bed. And ran over to the door. And started whining ... hnnnh! Hnnnh!

"You need to escape?" I asked her. "Are my choices that bad?"

And then I heard a noise.

ZWAK! ZWAK! And WHUF!

The door opened! And a big thing busted through the door making noises like ZWAK!

Rex! Zack's huge monstrous dog!

I love dogs, right? But Rex? He's not just any dog! He's a huge, wheezy, gooey, sneezy, messy dog.

Rex ran across my room! And oh nooooo! He was heading for my bed!

"No, Rex, nooooo!"

I tried to block him! But nooooo!

Rex jumped right on my bed!

On to all my clothes! He turned round and round. And rolled around ... on all of my outfits!!!

And then ...

ACHOO!

Rex sneezed. All over my yearbook outfits!

AUGH!!!!!!

And

GROSS!!!!!!

"Zack!" I yelled. "Get your dog out of my room!"

Zack ran in.

"Your dog got germy goo all over my yearbook outfits!" I screamed.

"Good job, Rex," Zack said.

"OUT!" I commanded. Zack dragged Rex out.

OK, now this was bad. All my choices. Totally ruined! Now what was I going to wear?!!!

Fashion crisis!

Knock, knock!

Someone knocked at my door. So I knew it wasn't Zack. He just busts right in.

"Maddy," Mom stuck her head in. "Phone! It's for you!"

She gave me the phone.

"Hi, Maddy, it's Lauren."

Lauren! From Limited Too! Whenever she called it meant something cool was about to happen!

"Hi, Lauren!" I said into the phone.

"We're about ready for the TOO Crew's next assignment," Lauren said. "I know this is very exciting. We're off to New York City."

Suuuu-weet!!!!!!

OK, get what happened. The TOO Crew helped out at this sleepover party! And we met the star who plays the prince in this new movie. The star was CARTER MCLAIN! He is #2 on my Ultimate Crush List! And I got to meet him in real and true life!

!!!!!!

AHHHHHH!!!!!!

And that's not even all. He told us we would get to go to New York City. And get to help out at a movie premiere!

I looooove movies. I love when I hear a new movie's coming out! I'm always like: Can I go see it right when it comes out?

And now ... how awesome is this going to be ...

A movie premiere!

I'll get to see a movie before anyone else!

I'll get to see the stars of the movie!!

Maybe I'll even see the red carpet!!!

In New. York. City!!!!!!

YEEEESSS! WOOHOO!

chapter 3

"We need to find Gate A14," my Dad said. My Dad and I were at the airport. On our way to the gate, on our way to our airplane, on our way to ...

NEW YORK CITY!!!

My Dad was going with me! He'd never been on a trip with me! But he's way into movies, too. OK, not princess movies like this one. But still! He wanted to come! And he can do some business stuff in New York, too.

"What did you put in this bag? This thing is heavy," my Dad was asking. He was carrying my suitcase. "Aren't we only going away for one night?"

Um, yes! But I had to bring lots of things. Here's what I packed:

- ★ 3 shirts
- ★ 1 poncho
- ★ 2 sweaters
- ★ 3 pairs of pants
- ★ 2 pairs of jeans
- ★ 1 skort
- ★ 1 skirt
- ★ 2 dresses

And 5 pairs of shoes.

OK, I packed too much! I know! But I was in a fashion crisis! Like, I didn't know what to wear for my yearbook picture. I also didn't know what to wear in New York City.

So I packed pretty much everything. Just in case.

I got the idea from yearbook day. Because for yearbook? I ended up wearing nothing special. Basically, I had to settle! For something that my brother's dog hadn't goo'ed all over.

That morning, when I sat down next to Brittany on the bus, I totally checked out her outfit. And I was psyched! She was wearing a white shirt. And jeans.

What was so cool about that?

I was wearing the same thing!!! The night before I thought ... at least it's safe! I know it matches. But I was worried it would be too boring.

But then I thought ... I guess I got it right! Because Fashionista Brittany was wearing the same thing!

But then ... listen to what happened.

When we went to the room where they were taking the yearbook pictures. Brittany came in with a rolling backpack. She said she wanted to see what the background looked like first. And then she'd choose from the three cool outfits she brought with her.

She checked out the background. She checked out what everyone else was wearing. And made her decision.

She even made the photographer wait while she changed into the right outfit. We all had to stand there in our lines waiting for her to change. Then Brittany came out in this cute little pleated skort and shirt and a hat.

I was still in the white shirt and jeans.

AUGH!!!!

So anyway. I learned my lesson! I'm doing the same thing. Bringing choices. Pretty much everything in my closet is with me on this trip. Great idea, huh?

"I think my arm is going to fall off." My Dad was not too happy. "I hope they let me carry these on."

"Uh, sorry. There's our gate!" I said. "You can put the bags down in a second."

I looked around to see if I could find the TOO Crew. I hadn't seen them since the sleepover!

And there they were!

KACEY! AND ISABEL! AND CLAIRE!!!

They were like, "Maddy! Maddy's heeeere!"

I ran over to them.

"I can't believe we're going to New York City!" Kacey screamed!

"I can't believe we're going to a movie premiere!" Isabel said.

"I can't believe we're going to see Carter McLain again!" Claire said.

We all were like ...

"AHHHHHHHH!!!!"

"I love New York," Isabel said. She and Claire had been there before. Isabel even had cousins there. But Kacey and me? First time for us!

"Here's a joke," Kacey said. "What's a dog's favorite city?"

We were like, "Um, what?"

"New Yorkie!" Kacey said. "Get it? 'Cuz of the dog called a

yorkie?"

We all were like, "Groan! Bad joke!"

"Mwah-ha-ha!" Kacey laughed.

"Er, may I ask what that sound was?" Lauren came over behind us.

"That was my evil laugh!" Kacey said. "Check it out. Mwah-ha-ha! Pretty evil, huh?"

Lauren agreed.

We were all like, "Hi Lauren!"

"I'm glad you're all here," Lauren told us. "We'll be boarding in a few minutes."

She said hi to my Dad.

"This works out well you came," she told him. "Isabel's father is here with us, too. And so is Bruno."

Bruno works for Claire's Dad. We all went over and said hi to Isabel's father and Bruno.

"It's nice to see you girls," Isabel's father said.

Isabel told us her father would be with us for part of the trip. And he would get to visit his sister, too, while we were doing TOO Crew stuff.

"I can't wait for my parents to come to something!" Kacey said. "It's taking forever to have my baby brother or sister! I can't wait much longer!"

Kacey's Mom is going to have a baby. So her parents have to stay around home. Just in case the baby comes!

"What if the baby comes tonight?" I said. Then I was like, oops! Maybe I shouldn't have said that. I don't want to worry her!

"Lauren made plans for that just in case!" Kacey laughed. "My parents thought that for one night it would be okay."

"Even for one night I'll miss my Buggie," I said. My little Bugaboo! Mom promised to feed Buggie her favorite beefy chewy treats! And squoosh up her blanket in the special way she likes. And make sure Rex didn't sneak all her food.

"But I brought a picture of her," I looked in my bag. I had made a pin with Buggie's picture in it. I stuck it to my pink newsboy hat.

"Awww! Cute little Buggie!" Claire said.

The announcements started.

"We're now boarding for our flight to New York. All passengers, all rows."

EEEE!!! I can't believe we're going to New York!

chapter 4

"What seat are you guys in?" Isabel asked. "I'm in 9A."

"8A!" Kacey said.

"8B, I'll be next to you," Claire said to her.

"And I'm in 9B," I said. Next to Isabel.

My Dad sat with Isabel's father and Bruno sat across the aisle. Lauren sat behind us. Isabel got the window seat.

"We can switch and share the window," Isabel told me.

"Thanks!" I said.

I like to look out the window! Floaty white clouds. Little tiny buildings. The buildings looking like Zack's race cars. I don't go on planes that much. Claire travels all the time with her father. All over the world!

We sat down. I buckled in. I made sure my seat was in the upright position. I made sure my tray was up. I was ready for takeoff.

Then I just sat there. Because here's the weird thing ...

I didn't know what to say! Isabel is part of the TOO Crew, right? So I mean she is totally my friend. Buuuut ... she is also so way cool. I mean, not only hip stylin cool, but also confident smart cool.

Like she never gets nervous (like me!)

Like she never does embarrassing things (like me!)

Like she never says anything stupid (OK! you get the picture!)

So even though I know we're friends, sometimes I'm like ...

UHHHHhhh.

What do I say? Something that doesn't sound dumb ...

"Are you going to get to see any of your cousins on the trip?" I asked her.

"Yeah! And listen to this," Isabel said. "Lauren said we have some free time. So one of my cousins is going to show us around the city. She's seriously cool. She's an art student at one of the colleges there."

"Cool!" I said. "So she's all artist like you are."

"Well, Sofia's a total artist. I'm just learning," Isabel said.

Isabel wants to be a fashion designer someday. And I know she will be. She has fashionista style. AND she is a majorly good drawer.

"I did get new supplies," Isabel said. She opened up her backpack and got out a black case.

KEWL!

Colored pencils! Oil pastels! Lots of colors. They were kinda fancy.

"Want to draw?" Isabel said.

"Sure! If you don't mind me using your stuff," I said.

Isabel held the case open. I picked out some colored pencils and paper.

"You guys want to draw?" Isabel asked Claire and Kacey. They all took some stuff and we started drawing.

The plane started to take off. It made all these noises and went up, up, up. Up to New York City!

I started to draw a picture of the movie premiere. A lot of red for a red carpet! I used yellow to make it look like flash bulbs. Like people taking pictures of all the stars.

And then I started to draw the two stars of the movie:

  ☆ Carter McLain and Starlize!

Carter McLain plays the prince. Starlize plays this regular girl who he totally falls for.

Ahhhh! Carter McLain!

How sweet would that be if Carter McLain was all like, "Maddy Sparks! I know you're a regular nobody girl with a bad hair day and no style! But you are my princess!"

So romantic. I mean, Carter McLain? Sooooo cute!

Not that you could tell from the picture I drew. His eyes were seriously googly.

OK, I'm not the greatest drawer. I won an art contest once. OK, it was in kindergarten. Meaning, "She colored inside the lines. And didn't eat the crayons."

The plane got a little bumpy.

"OOPS!" I said. I dropped the brown pencil. I leaned over to get it off the floor. And I saw this really cool silver case under Isabel's seat.

"That's really pretty," I said. "What kind of case is that?"

"Actually, it's my portfolio. It's a case for illustrations and things," Isabel said. "I have some of my designs I'm playing around with. I thought I could get inspired in New York."

"Can I see some of them?" I asked her.

Isabel looked kinda ... uncomfortable.

"Well, I really don't show them to anyone," she said all in a rush. "I mean, they're just practice stuff. I have a long ways to go. They're not really good."

Isabel was acting weird! Cool, confident Isabel was acting ... nervous. She put the picture she was drawing in the case. And closed it!

Um ...

I didn't mean to freak her out! What should I say?

Just then Claire leaned over the seat.

"May I have a brown pencil?" she asked. "I'm drawing a picture of my horse, Skydancer."

"Sure!" I said. I stuck my face in the art case. Saved!

"Hi guys!" Kacey leaned over the seat next to Claire. "Want to see my masterpiece? I call it: Kacey at the Bat. It's me playing softball. Our game was cancelled last night, though. Bummer. But we have another one Saturday and ..."

We were cracking up! Kacey is seriously talky!

"Could we please see the picture?" Isabel was laughing.

"Oh! Yeah!" Kacey said. She showed it to us. It was a smiling face with black hair. Holding a ... banana?

"I know! My bats look like bananas," Kacey sighed. But she was smiling. "Maddy, what are you drawing?"

"The movie premiere," I said. "But you guys don't want to see what I did to poor Carter McLain."

"Show us!" Kacey said.

OK! A little embarrassing. But after seeing Kacey's "bat" ...

I held up my picture.

"I like the red carpet," Claire said politely.

"But hee. Carter is kinda googly!" Kacey said. We cracked up.

"What were you drawing, Isabel?" Kacey asked her.

"I'm working on this design for a dress," Isabel said.

"Something you could wear to a movie premiere."

"Let's see!" said Kacey.

I looked at Isabel. I wondered what she'd say!

"OK. I have to confess something. I'm kinda nervous to show my designs to other people," Isabel said.

"Why?" I asked her. "I mean, you're such an awesome artist! You are so totally a fashion designer practically already!"

"Thanks, Maddy!" said Isabel. "That's cool of you to say it. But lately I've really been trying to make them good. I mean, being a fashion designer is my dream. What if someone looked at my best stuff. And went, What? This girl will never be a fashion designer!"

Wow! I never thought Isabel worried about anything!

"We understand," said Claire. "You don't have to show them to us."

Then Isabel took a deep breath.

"You know what?" Isabel said. She got her case from under the seat. "I should show you guys. I could use an honest opinion. And I know you guys won't make fun of them."

Of course not! Plus, I'm sure nobody ever makes fun of Isabel anyway!

She picked up her case. She took a deep breath and opened it and started flipping through her designs.

WHOA!!!!

There were these GORGEOUS pictures of outfits! Shirts, skirts, dresses, pants! All different colors! And not just like drawn stuff, but some of them had fabric and sequins and shiny stuff and beads she glued to them and ...

"Wow!" Kacey squealed. "These are way, way, way amazing!"

"They're beautiful," Claire said. "Truly."

"Isabel, you are such a fashion designer," I told her. "These are unbelievable."

Isabel looked embarrassed. But she was smiling.

"Thanks, you guys," she said. "But I know I've got a lot to learn. But I love making these."

She started to shut the case.

"Wait!" Kacey said. "I want to see that purple outfit again!"

We were all like, "Oooh! I like this one! I want to wear this! I love this!"

"Girls," Lauren leaned over from across the aisle to tell us something.

"Lauren!" I said. "You've got to see Isabel's ..."

"Maddy!" Isabel whispered. She shut the case. "I'm not ready for that, yet."

"But they're sooo good," I said. "And I mean, Lauren works in the fashion world! I bet she would love to see them!"

"Not ready," Isabel said, quietly. "But thanks anyway."

Lauren came over and sat in the empty seat next to me.

"I wanted to tell you more about the contest we held for this trip," Lauren said. And this is what she told us:

- ☆ There were 10 winners!
- ☆ They get a major shopping spree at Limited Too!
- ☆ They get to come to New York to see this movie premiere!
- ☆ They get to bring a friend (and a chaperone, of course)!
- ☆ They get to meet some of the stars!

Lauren told us we'd be helping with the movie premiere.

The premiere! I was so excited!

And, there was one thing I knew about the premiere. I'd brought the right outfit!

For once in my life I know my outfit is right! Here's how I know. One time we were on the bus and Brittany was looking through a magazine. It showed a movie premiere. And the actress was wearing this dress.

"This is sooo what I'm going to wear to MY movie premiere someday," Brittany had said. Brittany wanted to be a movie star ...

And a pop star ...

And a rock star! Pretty much anything with the word star in it.

So I quick peeked at it! I went and got that magazine when I went to the mall and found a dress that looked almost the same.

Anyway, that's what I will be wearing to the premiere! Exactly what Brittany and that actress would choose!

"Maddy? Did you catch that?" Lauren was saying.

Oh! Um ...

"Yes!" I said. "Actually no! Sorry. I was spacing out."

Lauren smiled.

"Just want to make sure everyone knows the schedule. You'll also have some time for sightseeing," Lauren said. "I know Isabel's cousin will be meeting us. And we'll get to see some of the sights of Manhattan."

"I can't wait to see the skyscrapers!" I said.

"I can't wait to see the Statue of Liberty!" Kacey said.

"I hope we get to see Central Park. It's so beautiful," Claire said.

"I hope we go by the garment district!" Isabel said.

?

"The what?" I asked her.

"The garment district. Maybe it sounds silly. It's this area where clothes are made," Isabel said. "Just being near it makes me feel like I'm around fashion from the very, very beginning."

"Spoken like a true future fashion designer," said Lauren.

Isabel smiled.

"You really should show her those designs," I whispered to Isabel. "Even Lauren thinks you're a future fashion designer."

Isabel was like, "SHUSH!"

"Of course we don't have time to do everything," Lauren was saying. "But you'll get a nice taste of New York."

OK. I'M SO EXCITED!!!! UH YEAH!!!!

I was bouncing in my seat! I was all like Kacey!

"Maybe you girls should relax quietly a little bit," Lauren suggested. "We have a busy day ahead of us."

Lauren went back to her own seat. My Dad was all talktalktalk to Isabel's Dad. Bruno was sleeping.

"How's cheerleading going?" Isabel asked me.

"Good!" I said. "We're going to have our first game when we get back. I'm kinda nervous. They put ME at the top of a pyramid!"

Kacey's head popped back over.

"Speaking of cheerleading," Kacey said. "What's a cheerleader's favorite color?"

"What?" I said.

"Yeller! Get it? Yell-er? Mwah-ha-ha!" she said.

"What's with all the jokes?" I asked.

"Well!" Kacey said. "Starlize got her start on that kids comedy show. Now she's a movie star!"

Kacey ... a comedian? Hey! Ya never know!

"My jokes need a little work, I know," Kacey told us. "I have a new joke book. I'll go find some new ones for ya."

Kacey sat back down. I could hear her flipping pages in a book ...

And cracking up!

Isabel pulled out a book, too.

"Ooh, I wanted to read that," I said, looking at it. "Is it good?"

"It's really good," Isabel said. "You can borrow it when I'm finished if you want."

"Thanks," I said.

I needed something to do. I got out my diary. I flipped it open to the page I left off. A page on style called ...

Stylometer

Where are you in the fashion world? (check one)

- ☐ Ultimate Fashion Guru
- ☐ Super Style Princess
- ☐ Oh So Trendy
- ☑ Plain Jane

I think I have great fashion sense when it comes to:

- ☐ shoes
- ☐ accessories
- ☐ dressing up
- ☐ dressing down
- ☐ other people
- ☐ everything
- ☐ school attire
- ☑ only in my dreams

Blugh. I have about ZERO style.

"What?" Isabel looked up from her book.

Did I say that out loud?

"Did you say something about style?" Isabel said.

"Yeah," I confessed. "That I don't have any. Even the diary proves it. Look. I'm a 'Plain Jane' who has style 'only in her dreams.'"

"Maddy, that's not exactly true," Isabel said.

"It's true. Face it! I never know what to wear. Yearbook pictures? I panicked. I ended up in a boring white shirt with jeans. Exactly the outfit Brittany changed out of."

Isabel cracked up a little.

"And also," I said. "I think I even blinked. I'm so doomed."

I looked at Isabel. She was wearing a striped poncho, a cool hat and jeans with pins stuck in them. Total hip chick.

Kacey was bouncing around in her seat, listening to headphones. Kacey was wearing a grey hoodie and matching flippy scooter. So sporty cute.

Claire was reading. She was wearing a black and pink polka dot top and skirt. So pretty. As always.

Totally different styles. But at least they had one! OK. I needed to think about something else. I turned to the next page of my diary.

Every girl needs a fun tee with a super cute saying. Mine

would say ...

OK, what would mine say?

Isabel's would say: Sooo cool!

Kacey's would say: SportyGirl!

Claire's would say: Princess

Mine would say, ummm ...

Confused!

Auk!!

Then Isabel unbuckled her seat belt.

"I almost forgot, Maddy," she said. "We should switch so you get the window!"

We switched seats. I saw the puffy clouds. And then I started to see the ground.

An announcement came on ...

"We are beginning our final descent into New York. Please put your trays in an upright position and ..."

Ohmigosh.

I'm almost in NEW YORK CITY!!!!

"Do you want to switch back?" I asked Isabel. "I think we're going to see the city stuff soon!"

"That's OK. It's your first time so you've gotta see it!"

I watched the ground go by. I could start to see little cars and stuff on the ground. But no city yet ... not yet ... but then ...

Ohmigosh!

OH. MY. GOSH!

You could see water below with boats all around ... and then the plane turned and we could see ...

NEW. YORK. CITY!

Tons of skyscrapers!

"There's the Statue of Liberty!" Kacey squealed.

Isabel was leaning over me looking out the window. "There's the Empire State Building!" Isabel pointed.

I saw an airport below and ...

We were LANDING!!!!

In New York City!!!!

chapter 5

This Journal Belongs to:

Maddy Elizabeth Sparks

I'm here! I'm waiting in the lobby of the hotel! With Kacey! And Isabel! And Claire! And Lauren. Our hotel is in Times Square. Yes! The Times Square you watch on New Year's Eve! With the ball dropping down.

You should see the view from my window. It's like this:

★ Flashing signs advertising stuff!

★ Giant TV screens showing the news and stuff!

★ Traffic! (The cars are like honk! Honk! Beep!)

★ And people, zillions of people, walking around everywhere!

Well, off we go. We're going to start helping out. First, we are going to help out decorating for the premiere!

The premiere is being held at a big movie theater. We are going to help set up! Because it is going to be ...

FANCY!

Oh, Lauren's saying something to me.

G2g

"Maddy, I'd like a lot of pictures taken on this trip," Lauren said. "I know you like photography. So I'm putting you in charge of the digital camera. Feel free to take pictures along the way."

Kewl!

I took the camera bag. I put it over my shoulder. I felt kinda like a real photographer!

"We'll grab a taxi to take us to the theater," Lauren said. "Let's go!"

We left the hotel lobby. And went out the front doors. And through the double doors into the streets of ...

TIMES SQUARE!

Ohmigosh! I jumped back. There were like six kabazillion people walking on the sidewalk. Not just walking! Rushing! Really fast!

"I never saw so many people in my life!" Kacey said.

"About 8 million people live here," Lauren said. "And more than 30 million people visit here each year! A lot of people walking around! But we have a little ways to go. So we'll catch a cab."

Isabel stepped out near the curb. And all of a sudden there was this noise!

TWEEET!

It was Isabel whistling! And sticking up her hand! And a yellow taxi pulled right up in front of us!

"Wow, that was cool!" I said.

"My cousins taught me that move," Isabel said. We all slid into the backseat. Put on our seat belts. Lauren told the driver where to take us.

And the taxi was like, Vroom! Then Stop. Then Vroom!

I looked out the window. It was like store after store after store. So many buildings! So many people!

"Here's a joke," Kacey said. "Who earns a living driving their customers away?"

We were like, "Who?"

"A taxi driver!" Kacey said.

"Hey. I heard that," the taxi driver said.

We were like ... "Uh! Was he mad?"

Nope. He was smiling.

"That was a pretty good one," the taxi driver said. "Here's one. Who rides in a taxi but doesn't pay?"

We were like, "Who?"

"The driver!" he said.

We all were like, "Groan!"

"We are here!" the taxi driver said.

We pulled up to this theater.

The sign out front said:

```
WORLD MOVIE PREMIERE
      TONIGHT!
```

WOOHOO!

We got out of the cab and went inside. It was a big movie theater with a huge screen. There were some people walking around and setting up some things. We followed Lauren up to the front.

"As you know, this is going to be a premiere for *The Princess Movie*," Lauren said. "We will want our contest winners to feel special and princess-like. Our winners get to sit in this section, right up front near the movie stars."

She showed us an area that was roped off. Front row!

"Hello." This girl came over to us. "Who are you?"

Lauren introduced us as the TOO Crew. We all said hi.

And waited.

"And you are ...?" Lauren asked.

"I'm Janice," she said. "I'm an assistant to the designers of the movie. My specialty is fashion design. I helped with the costuming of the movie."

"Cool," said Isabel.

"Can you direct me to who is in charge?" Lauren asked her.

"Of course," Janice said.

She pointed to a woman across the room. Lauren thanked her and walked over.

"I can't believe that woman over there is my boss," Janice said to us. "She's like the same age as me. I should have been the boss of this job. I'm way better. But whatever."

Oooookay. Janice looked not too happy.

So ... Um.

"Isabel wants to be a fashion designer someday," I said. "Do you like it?"

Janice gave Isabel that look. You know, like up and down. Checking her out.

"Well, I'm on the verge of my big break," Janice said. "I graduated from college and I'm just doing this lowly assistant thing between jobs. It's really quite below my skill level. And certainly my talent level."

"Well, good luck," Claire said.

"With my talent, I won't need luck," the girl sniffed. And walked away.

Oooook! We all looked at each other. That girl was r-u-d-e!

"Maybe we should go find Lauren," I said. We went over to Lauren.

"We're ready to get you girls to work," Lauren said. "First, it would be helpful if you'd decorate these seats for our winners and their guests. We have some supplies for you here. Use your creativity! Just be sure to put their names on the backs of them."

She gave us a list of the winners' names. And some silvery shiny cardboard stuff. Thick pretty markers. Glitter glue!

Sparkly confetti!

"What should we make?" I asked.

"How about princess crowns with their names on them?" Kacey said.

"Yup, perfect," Isabel said. "Claire, your handwriting is so neat. Could you write the names?"

"Isabel has got to decorate them," I said. "I'll cut."

"I'll stick 'em to the backs of the seats!" Kacey said. I started cutting crown shapes. Claire started writing the winners' names and where they were from.

- ☆ Ariel - Minnesota
- ☆ Katie - Florida
- ☆ Kayley - Oregon
- ☆ Kelly - Illinois
- ☆ Laura - Indiana
- ☆ Xiomara - Texas
- ☆ Cassie - Nebraska
- ☆ Erika - Georgia
- ☆ Angie - Connecticut
- ☆ Megan - New Jersey

"Cool," I said. "All these states all over the country. The girls must be excited!"

Every winner got to bring a friend and a parent. So I was like, cut cut cut.

"Here's a joke," Kacey said. "Why did Cinderella get kicked off the soccer team? Because she ran away from the ball! Mwah-ha-ha!"

We all were like, "Boo! Groan!" But we were all smiling.

"Here are some pink and silver streamers," Isabel said. "Could look cool if we wrap the chairs, like this."

"So, you girls are from here?"

It was Janice. She came over to us. Maybe she was getting friendlier?

"No, we're just visiting," Isabel said.

"Maddy and I have never been here before!" Kacey said. "It's so exciting!"

"Oh, that's so touristy," Janice sniffed. "I grew up here." She rolled her eyes. Then she changed and got all smiley. Lauren was walking over.

"Lauren!" Janice said. All nice and icky-sweet. "I was just telling these girls what a fab job they did on the decorations."

She was?

"You are doing a nice job, TOO Crew," Lauren said. "I think it's really going to look festive. I like what they've done to the stage."

"Did you hear about the actor who fell through the floor?" Kacey asked. "It was just a stage he was going through. Mwah-ha-ha!"

"Boo!" We booed her. But we were laughing.

"Isabel, look who's here," Lauren said.

And then Isabel goes ...

"SOFIA!"

Isabel's cousin was here! She had black hair cut really short. She was wearing a funky long shirt and long skirt and long dangly earrings. She ran over and gave Isabel a big hug.

"Izzy!" she screamed. Isabel introduced the TOO Crew. And Sofia gave us each a big hug! She was so nice already!

"I'm so excited to show you guys around New York," Sofia said. "I've lived here all my life. But I still never get tired of this city!"

"This is Maddy and my's first time," Kacey said. "We're really excited."

"That is exciting!"

She was way nicer than Janice. She didn't roll her eyes and be like ugh, tourists.

"Isabel is my kindred spirit, right?" Sofia said, hugging her. "She's going to follow in her favorite cousin's footsteps in fashion design, right? Izzy, have you been working on anything?"

"You should see her portfolio!" I bursted out. "It's awesome!"

"Izzy, let me see it!" Sofia said.

"OK," Isabel went and got her silver portfolio. Sofia started looking through it. You could tell Sofia was like ...

Wow! These are really good!

I went back to cutting crowns. Cut Cut Cut ...

"You did those?" Janice was asking Sofia. Janice had come over and was looking over Sofia's shoulder at the portfolio.

"Actually, Isabel did," Sofia said. "Can you believe that? She's got an eye already."

Janice was all, Hmph! Rolling her eyes again!

But then Janice's eyes got big! She was like ...

GASP!

And she pointed ...

"Look! Paulinna is here!"

Everyone looked. This woman was walking in. Way glam in her long cape. Surrounded by lots of people. Buzzing around her.

Is that Paulinna? The famous fashion designer? Even I knew who she was!

"Paulinna designed the outfits in the movie. Pure genius! And she designed the dress Starlize is wearing tonight to the premiere!" Janice said, all excited. "But I didn't know she was coming here!"

"Wow," Isabel said. "I can't believe I am seeing her in real life! She's one of my idols!"

Isabel looked way excited! Paulinna was looking around at everything. The people around her were taking notes.

"Those must be her assistants," Isabel said. "What a dream

job."

"Looks like a reporter, too," Kacey added. "See the guy with the tape recorder?"

Paulinna was walking toward the front rows. She put her finger to her chin.

"The dress!" she was saying loudly to the people around her. "Will be perfect in this venue! It is silver colored! But with the subtle hint of metallic steel. Much like ..."

She looked around. Then she looked our way.

"That silver, there!"

Paulinna waved her hand our way. And started walking over to our section.

"Excuse me!" Paulinna called out. "You, with the silver case. May I see that for one moment, please."

"This?" Sofia asked. She held up Isabel's portfolio.

"Correct," Paulinna said. She took the portfolio and started talking to the man with the tape recorder. "You must instruct your photographer to be prepared for a silver dress similar to this color. Against the red carpet, the glints of light will be spectacular."

"I can't believe Paulinna is touching my portfolio!" Isabel said really quiet to us. "Eeee!"

And then ... it happened.

Paulinna was waving the portfolio around. And it kinda ... opened.

"Oh no!" Sofia said. "I didn't zipper it all the way!"

Isabel's designs started slipping out. Paulinna kept talking! And then the zipper busted open! And the portfolio fell open!

And paper was flying everywhere! Isabel's designs! Paulinna looked down.

We were like ...

Ooops. Nobody said anything. Then all the assistants were quick quick! Pick them up! No problemo!

But Paulinna said, "STOP!"

She leaned over. She picked up one of the papers.

"You!" she said to Sofia. "Is this your work?"

"Actually, they're my cousin Isabel's," Sofia said to Paulinna.

"Aha! Cousin Isabel!" Paulinna pronounced. "Cousin Isabel must come to my office at 3 p.m. today. I will apologize to her in person for mixing up her work."

I started to point to Isabel. Like, this is her! Cousin Isabel is here! But Paulinna kept talking so we couldn't tell her!

"And Cousin Isabel must bring her portfolio!" Paulinna said. "And now I must go!"

And she turned and whirled away! Her assistants whirled off, too.

I could hear her saying to the reporter: "Make sure you put in the story how Paulinna is helping young unknowns with their dreams ..."

We were all like, "WHOA!"

"OK, what just happened?" Isabel was all in a daze.

chapter 6

"Izzy! Paulinna is going to look at your designs!" Sofia was jumping up and down. "This is huge! This is astronomical! This is ..."

"Not going to happen," Isabel said. "I can't show her these! They're just practice! I'm not ready!"

Isabel looked kind of upset! She was all shaky! I never saw her like that, before! Ever!

"You have to go!" I said. "This is so major!"

"I just can't," Isabel said. "What if she hates them! What if she says I have no future!"

"If you're chickening out, I'll go in your place," Janice said. "I'll pretend to be Cousin Isabel."

"No you won't," Sofia said. "Isabel will be there with her fabulous portfolio."

Janice was not happy.

But then, whew! Lauren came over.

"Did you girls see Paulinna?" Lauren asked us.

"Oooh ya! And you're not going to believe what happened!" Kacey said.

"They're closing this room for a bit," Lauren said. "So why don't you tell me while we're sightseeing."

We said goodbye to everyone. Including Janice! Buh-bye!

"We're going to be full-out tourists," Lauren said. "I've got us tickets on a sightseeing bus. It will take us all over the city." Kewl!

We walked outside.

"Now, you're not used to these streets," Lauren cautioned. "Watch for the walk and don't walk signs when you're crossing."

We walked a couple blocks to the bus place. There were cars! People! Everywhere!

This bus rolled up. But not just any bus. A double decker bus! You could sit on the bottom inside, like a regular bus. Or you could sit upstairs where there was no roof!

"Do you want to sit inside or on the top?" Lauren asked.

"TOP!" We all yelled. We all raced up the stairs and grabbed seats. We all grabbed seats next to each other. Me, Kacey, Claire, Isabel, Sofia and Lauren.

"This is cool," I said. We seemed high up off the street!

"Welcome to your tour of Manhattan!" the tour guide said. He told us Manhattan was an island, and only one part of New York City, along with the Bronx, Queens, Brooklyn and Staten Island.

"I brought the camera!" I said. I got ready to take pictures of everything.

And we were off!

"Look! It's Broadway!" Claire said. "Where the plays and musicals are! My Dad and I have so much fun at the shows!"

"Act Broadwayish!" I commanded. Claire posed like a dancer. I took her picture with some of the signs for the musicals behind them.

CLICK!

"That's Madison Square Garden," Sofia pointed out. "Where sports events and concerts are."

"Wow! That's where they play basketball! Hockey! Even the WBNA plays there!" Kacey was bouncing all over. She pretended to shoot a basket.

"Swish!" she said. I took a picture.

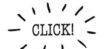
CLICK!

"I'm gonna frame that picture!" Kacey said.

I bet Kacey will even play here someday! She's awesome at basketball!

The tour guide told everyone to look up. It was the Empire State Building! The bus stopped.

"We can get out and go to the top if you'd like," Lauren said. "Anyone?"

"Yeah!" Isabel said, getting up.

"Yes!" Kacey said.

Uh ... I wasn't so sure. I looked at Claire. She looked at me like ... Um ... we were like ...

That building is tall! I was a little freaky about it.

"I'll try it," Claire said.

I took a deep breath. OK. I would do it.

"We can come down if you don't like it," Isabel reassured me.

OK! I would do it! I would close my eyes if it was too nervousing.

We went into the lobby and got tickets.

"We're lucky there's no long line," Sofia said. We got in the elevators.

Observation Deck ... 86th floor!

We went Up ...

Up ...

Up!

We got out and ...

WOW!!!!

"Wow," Isabel said. "You can see all over the place!"

We all ran over to the binocular things that you could look through.

I looked at Claire next to me. She was closing her eyes!

"You OK?" I asked her.

"I'm a little nervous," Claire admitted. "Tell me what you see."

"I can see skyscrapers! And boats on the water! Some huge bridges! You can see way far! It's like you can see forever!"

"You can see New Jersey, Pennsylvania, Connecticut, and Massachusetts from up here," Sofia told us.

Then I looked down toward the ground. It made me dizzy for a second.

"The cars on the street are so tiny," I said. "It's like people are little ants."

"Speaking of ants," Kacey said. "Where do ants eat? A restaurant! Get it? Restaur-ant?"

Isabel and I groaned.

But Claire was laughing! And now she had her eyes open.

"Ohmigosh," Claire said, looking around. "It is beautiful! I'm glad I looked. I'm not nervous anymore."

"We should probably continue our tour," Lauren said.

"Yeah, we want to make sure we don't miss Isabel's meeting with Paulinna!" Sofia said.

"Alright, now I'M nervous," Isabel said. "We can just skip that. Do more sightseeing."

"No way!" I said. "You have to go!"

"I'm sure she doesn't take time to meet with that many people," Sofia said.

"I hope she doesn't think she's wasting her time," Isabel said.

We went back down the elevator.

Down ...

Down ...

Down!

"I can't believe we were 86 floors up!" Kacey said. We went back on one of the double deckers and grabbed upstairs seats. Of course!

The bus started going again.

"That's Rockefeller Center," Sofia pointed out.

"My Dad took me ice skating there," Claire said. "It's neat."

We were all like, "Look at that! Look!" Pointing at everything.

"We're coming up on Madison Avenue," the tour bus guy said. "Fifth Avenue and Madison Avenue are famous for ..."

SHOPPING!!!!

Wow! It was like storestorestorestore. Beautiful gold and sparkling fancy stores.

"Do you shop there a lot?" I asked Sofia.

"Nah. I'm on a student budget," she laughed. "Anyway, my style is a little more downtown, more funky. The Village, Soho, that kind of thing. What kind of style do you think you'd be?"

"Ugh," I said. "Don't ask. I have no style."

Before she could say anything back, Isabel said, "Look!"

We all looked.

I saw a huge building with two ginormous lion statues in front of it.

"That's the New York Public Library," Sofia said. "Imagine how many books are in there!"

Kewl!

I took a picture of Isabel with the lions behind her.

CLICK!

"What else do you do in the city when you visit?" I asked Claire and Isabel.

"My father takes me to a lot of museums," Claire said. "The Metropolitan Museum has all these famous paintings and statues and things. The American Museum of Natural History has all these animals and dinosaurs and things. Sometimes we see classical music, ballets, things like that."

"I like to shop. Of course!" Isabel said. "And also, my cousins always take me on a food fest! New York City is way famous for food. Chinatown, Little Italy, bagels ..."

"You're making me hungry!" I told her.

"We should probably skip the sit-down lunch," Lauren said. "How about a hot dog from a street vendor?"

We got off the bus. Lauren went over to the cart and ordered hot dogs and drinks.

I got a hot dog with ketchup!

Kacey got a hot dog with mustard!

Claire got a hot dog with nothing on it!

Isabel got a hot dog with pickle relish.

Pickle relish? Ek.

We all sat on a bench and totally chowed our hot dogs.

"Why didn't the hot dog star in the movies?" Kacey asked. "Because the rolls weren't good enough! Mwah-ha-ha!"

We all were like, "Groan!"

"What's the only kind of dog you can eat?" Kacey asked.

We all knew this one!

"A hot dog!" we yelled. And then we all yelled ...

"MWAH-HA-HA!"

"Girls, girls, girls," Lauren said, shaking her head. "We'll need to head back to the theater. The winners will be arriving!"

"We're right near a subway station," Sofia said. "It might be fastest to take the subway. No traffic."

"Let's do it!" Isabel said. "The subway is pretty cool."

We went down the stairs to a subway station. Lauren got us tokens and we stuck them through the turnstile thingies.

"It's really cool to go in the front car. You can see everything," Isabel said.

We went to the front of the train. The subway started moving! We were going really fast! It looked so dark in the tunnel! Except when sparks would fly! It was pretty cool.

"This is our stop," Lauren said. "Everybody off!"

chapter 7

We were in the theater! Lauren wanted to greet the winners of the contest when they arrived. They were coming to the theater first to meet one of the movie stars.

"The winners are coming! The winners are coming!" Kacey was all jumping up and down.

We were so excited for the winners! We already knew their names! From making their crowns. But I knew how so totally cool it would be to win a contest to come to NYC! For a movie premiere!

Lauren had asked us to say hi to the winners. To welcome them to New York! To congratulate them for winning the contest! She also wanted us to take pictures. They were going to put the pictures up on a website.

A bunch of girls and their families came in! Lauren was all talking to them. We went over and were like, "Hi! Hi! Hi! Welcome! Welcome! Congratulations! Congratulations!"

"I can't believe I'm in New York City!" one of the girls said. "I live in a small town!"

"I'm so excited for the movie premiere," another girl said.

"Do you think we'll really get to see Carter McLain and Starlize?" another girl asked.

Everyone was all EEEEEEEEEEEEEEEEEE!!!!

I remembered my job! OK! Picture time!

"Can all the winners stand together? I can get a group shot." I said.

Everyone skooched in together.

All the girls were wearing t-shirts that said the name of the movie on them. They were all jumping around and happy to see their names on the seats. Like, we can't believe we're front row at a movie premiere!

"OK! Everyone smile," I got ready to take the picture.

I focused my camera. Everyone was smiling ... OK, get ready and ...

"Say cheese!" I told them.

"Carter McLain!" everyone said.

Huh? Nobody was smiling. They all had their mouths open looking kinda dazed or something.

"OK, you can say Carter," I told them. "You don't have to say cheese. But you have to smile."

All the girls were all like, "No! look!"

I turned around and ... ohmigosh!

Standing right behind me.

It was Carter McLain! THE Carter McLain, star of the movie!

Everyone was like **"AHHHHHHHHHHHHHHHH!!!!!!!"**

Everyone crowded around him.

"Anyone want an autograph?" Carter said.

"YEAH!!!"

His manager asked everyone to line up. He got out a pen and the winners were all like, "AHHHHH!!! Eeeeee!"

"Excuse me, TOO Crew people?" Janice said. "I could use some workers to mop the floors and scrub the seats. So, I thought you guys could ..."

"Actually, we're just taking off soon," Sofia said.

"What does she think we are?" Kacey whispered. "Her

Cinderellas?"

"Going to your appointment with Paulinna?" Janice asked. "Aren't you special?"

She walked away. With this look on her face like she was way jealous.

"If that girl was nicer, I'd offer to bring her with us. But yeesh," Sofia said. "Where is Isabel anyway?"

"She's talking to some of the contest winners!" Kacey said. "They all get to pick out outfits to wear tonight from Limited Too clothes. One of the girls was all worried about which outfit she should wear. So Isabel is helping. That girl knows her fashion!"

"I can't wait for her to show her portfolio to a famous designer," I said. "That's so cool!"

"Her portfolio is right here," Sofia said. "Keep an eye on it for me. I'm going to find Lauren and then we'll head to Paulinna's studio. I can't wait just to see that!"

Sofia went looking for Lauren.

"Oh, there's Lauren," Kacey said. "I'll go tell her Sofia's looking for her." She took off to the other side of the theater.

I watched the contest winners get autographs.

"Duh!" I said. "I should take a picture of the girls with Carter! That would be perfect for the website!"

I picked up the camera. I took a couple of shots of the girls in line. Then I asked if they would all line up. Carter stood in the middle. The girls were all hee hee hee!

"OK, smile!" I said.

 CLICK!

Kacey, Isabel and Claire came over. So did Sofia and Lauren.

"OK, gang, we're ready to go to Paulinna's studio," Lauren said.

"I think I'm finally calm enough," Isabel said. "I'm just going to do it!"

"Go, Isabel!" we all cheered.

I got my denim bag.

Kacey got her backpack.

Claire got her pink C bag.

Isabel got her messenger bag.

"Who's got my portfolio?" Isabel asked.

"Maddy has it," Sofia said.

Um. Except I didn't. I put it on the chair when I took the picture.

"It's on that chair," I said, pointing.

Isabel went over.

"No, not on the chair."

"Check around," Sofia said. "Maddy, you sure that's where you put it?"

"Positive," I said. I ran over.

No portfolio!

Everyone was looking around.

"Excuse me!" Lauren said in a loud voice. "We're looking for a silver case. It has important papers in it. Can everyone take a look around, please?"

Everyone in the theater stopped and started looking around.

I got on my knees. I looked underneath the seats.

NOTHING!

"Check the stage area," Claire suggested.

"Check behind the curtain," Janice said.

Everyone was like, "Check here! Check here!"

"My portfolio is gone," Isabel said.

Oh.

No.

This can't be happening.

chapter 8

"I am so, so, so sorry," I kept saying. We'd given up looking for the portfolio. We'd looked everywhere!

Kacey had to go to the bathroom. Claire went with her. Usually we'd all go in there together. And joke about the time we met and got locked in the bathroom.

But nobody was in a joking mood, now!

"Don't worry about it, Maddy," Isabel said. "It's probably just a sign, anyway. A sign my stuff isn't good enough. A sign I'm not supposed to go see Paulinna."

"Your portfolio IS good enough!" I told her. "It's my stupid fault."

I couldn't figure it out! I know I was supposed to be watching it! But I didn't go very far! Where could it have gone?!!!

I'd screwed up things before. I'd embarrassed myself a bajillion times. But this ...

It was like I was ruining Isabel's life!!! How often do you get a famous fashion designer to give you advice?!!!

Like, never. So Isabel had to go at least meet her!

"Come on," I told her. "You need to go anyway."

"No, I'm just going to cancel," Isabel said.

"Isabel! What do you always tell me when I'm worried about doing something?"

"Maddy!" Isabel said.

"You say ... just go for it!" I reminded her.

"And to just be confident in yourself," Isabel admitted. "And to try your best. I know, I know."

"And what does Starlize say to Prince Carter McLain in the movie trailer?" I asked.

"A true princess follows her dreams," Isabel said. She was kinda smiling.

"So come on," I said. "Let's get Sofia and everyone. Let's just go."

"Oh, alright," Isabel said. "I guess if I use those lines on you, I better do it, huh?"

I went into the bathroom. Kacey and Claire were looking at

me like, how is she?

"Isabel's going to see Paulinna!" I yelled. "Hurry! Before she changes her mind!"

We were like, "YEAH!"

OK, no portfolio! But at least Isabel would get to meet with her!

"I'll get a cab!" Sofia said.

chapter 9

So we got to Paulinna's studio. Lauren took Isabel to the security desk to check her in. The rest of us waited outside.

I was still pretty bummed! Mad at myself! Isabel worked so hard on that portfolio. Where could it have gone?

"Cheer up, Maddy!" Kacey said.

"It'll be okay," Claire said. She looked around. "It's pretty over here."

Paulinna's office was right next to Central Park.

"Let's go for a little walk," Sofia said. "So we're not just standing here, worrying."

"Well, at least you're getting to see Central Park like you wanted," I told Claire.

"This is so cool!" Kacey said. "It's like one minute you're in this huge city and then, BAM! You're out in the country or something!"

It was really pretty. All naturey. We walked past a pond. And all these people rollerblading and running. There was some race going on. All these people wearing numbers were running by us. People were cheering them on.

"Go racers!" Kacey cheered. "I love when people do that at my track meets."

"There's a great rollerskating rink over there," Sofia pointed. "It's an ice skating rink in the winter. And some baseball fields and tennis ..."

"Oo ya," Kacey said. "I'm liking this park!"

"There's also a lake with boats on it," Claire said. "Playgrounds. And a zoo! I've even ridden horses with my father here!"

"I hope you guys come back soon, so we can do even more things," Sofia said. She sat down on the lawn.

I sat down near everyone. But I was really bummed out! Couldn't stop thinking about Isabel. I put down my backpack. I kept it really close to me! I didn't want to lose anything else. Like my new camera!

I still felt like it was my fault! I checked to make sure I hadn't already lost the camera, too.

I opened up the camera case. I remembered a time at my BFF Taylor's birthday party. By accident, I had opened the film thing on my camera. And all the pictures were ruined! I was so upset.

I should check the pictures I'd been taking here. I didn't want those ruined, too! I flipped through.

There was Kacey, pretending to shoot a basket outside Madison Square Garden!

There was Claire, in front of Broadway posing like an actress!

There was Isabel, talking to Paulinna! She was so happy!

Then there were all the contest winners in line with Carter! Smiling! That was a good photo. It was a little off, though. Too much background.

I zoomed in. I could crop out the right part. And the picture would look more balanced. I zoomed in more. And then I saw something weird.

Contest winners smiling. Carter McLain smiling. Janice in the background not smiling.

And Janice was holding something ... something shiny ...

Wait a minute.

I zoomed in closer. It looked kinda silverish.

I clicked to the next picture. There Janice was again. And she was putting something in her tote bag. I zoomed in more.

It WAS silver!

It was Isabel's portfolio!

OH!

MY!!

GOSH!!!

Janice took Isabel's portfolio.

I had to tell Lauren! I had to tell Isabel! Kacey was showing Sofia and Claire her handstand.

"Sofia! I have something to show you!" I yelled.

She came over.

"Sofia! We have to get back to Paulinna's office!" I quick explained what was in the pictures.

"Are you sure?" Sofia asked me.

"Look!" I yelled. I showed her the pictures.

"Whoa," Sofia said. "You're right." She got out her cell phone and dialed.

"Hi, Lauren," Sofia said. Then she listened. "The guard won't let you in? He said someone was already there for the appointment?"

Someone was already there ...

Wait a minute. Janice stole Isabel's portfolio. Maybe she stole her appointment, too?

"Sofia! Tell Lauren to wait!" I screamed.

"Oh, no! My battery went dead," Sofia said. "But you know what. We may still have a chance. Let's go. And FAST!"

"Kacey! Claire! Hurry! No time to explain! We have to go to Isabel!" I yelled to them.

Kacey and Claire came running.

"Come on! Let's go!"

We started running through the park. As fast as we could! We were faster than the joggers! Faster than the rollerbladers!

Past the rink!

Past the pond!

To the exit of the park!

Could we make it in time to explain?

All of a sudden the racing people were running by. I was running in a line of racers!

"Excuse me!" I gasped. "Excuse me!" I ran with them! Ran right by them!

I ran and ran! All these people were cheering on the racers.

"Go! Go!" They were yelling.

I was! I had to win the race! The race against time! The race for Isabel's portfolio! Go, Maddy, go!

"Go, girl in the dog shirt!" I heard someone yell.

"Is that girl winning the marathon?" I heard some kid ask.

I ran past them! Kacey, Claire and Sofia were right behind me!

And then I heard Sofia yell, "The blinking sign has the don't walk signal ..."

We had to stop and wait! Hurry, light, change!

And the sign changed! The hand was like WALK!

"Careful crossing!" Sofia said. We all crossed the street.

"OK, now run!" Sofia commanded. We ran past the other people.

"Excuse me! Pardon me!" Claire was saying as she ran by.

We reached the building. We were all totally out of breath!

Oh no! Lauren and Isabel were walking out through the revolving doors!

Were we too late?!!!!

"Security said we can't go in there," Isabel said. "Figures. I knew it was too good to be true."

"Don't give up yet," I told her. I ran over to Lauren.

"Wait! Don't leave yet!" I yelled.

"Sorry, Maddy," Lauren said. "The security guard said her appointment already arrived. Very odd."

"Lauren! I think I know what's going on! I think it might be Janice in there! Stealing Isabel's appointment!" I was all rushed!

"Maddy, what are you talking about?" Lauren said.

I held up the camera. Lauren looked at the picture. I showed her the next one.

"Lauren! Janice took Isabel's portfolio! And now she's probably in there with Paulinna! Pretending it's hers!"

"Oh my," Lauren said. "Excuse me for one moment, girls. I need to have a word with the security guard."

We ran back to Kacey, Claire and Sofia. I quick told Kacey and Claire what the picture showed.

They were like, "GASP!"

"I can't believe it," Isabel said. "This is crazy."

"That Janice girl is just plain awful," Sofia said. "I hope Lauren can fix the situation."

We were all waiting in the lobby! Ohmigosh! Could Lauren get to Paulinna in time?

Lauren came out! With the security guard.

"Please do come in," he said to us.

"We'll wait outside. This is really Isabel's meeting," Claire said.

"After all this?" Isabel said. "No way! You guys are my support! I need you!"

Then she looked at me.

"Especially Maddy."

Isabel needed ... me?

Let's go!

The assistant led us through the door. We went through a hall.

Wow! This was some office! It was huge and everything was white. There was a big desk and in the chair was ...

"Paulinna!" Isabel breathed.

And in front of her was ... Janice. Janice was leaning over the desk. And she was showing Paulinna ...

ISABEL'S PORTFOLIO!!

"Excuse me," Paulinna said to Janice. "We have more guests."

Janice turned around. And her face was like ...

UH.

OH.

"Uh ... what are these children doing interrupting our meeting?" Janice stammered."You should probably call security ..."

Then Lauren walked in. Janice stopped talking.

"It seems we have a little mixup here," Paulinna stated. "Perhaps there has been some confusion. I invited the owner of this portfolio to meet with me today."

She looked at Janice.

"Is this your work?"

Janice was like ... GULP.

"OK, here's the deal," Janice said. "I want to be a designer real bad. OK, so maybe this isn't exactly my portfolio. But you can't blame me for jumping at this opportunity to get advice from you. I mean, you're the famous Paulinna!"

"That is correct," Paulinna said. "And I became the famous Paulinna because of my own ideas. My own styles. My own designs. Not because I stole someone else's."

Janice was like ... "Uh ..."

"I am going to let you off easy. You are young. You are foolish.

I hope you've learned a lesson. You will never, ever be a fashion designer if you try to pass off other peoples' work as your own. And you will only cheat yourself if you copy someone else's styles."

Janice started to slink out of the room.

"Are you not owing someone an apology?" Paulinna called after her.

"Sorry," Janice mumbled to Isabel.

And then Janice bolted! Outta there!

"That was unpleasant," Paulinna said. "But I wanted to share that lesson with all of you girls. And now I would like to take a few moments with the young lady of the portfolio."

Isabel went up to her desk.

The rest of us walked out.

"Did you see Janice's face?" Kacey asked. "Youch! She was so busted."

"Whew! A mystery solved! A chase scene! That was just like in the movies," Sofia said.

Claire gave me a big hug. "Maddy, you saved the day!"

This Journal Belongs to:

Maddy Elizabeth Sparks

OK! Here we are in the lobby of Paulinna's office. Waiting for Isabel to come out. This is all so way crazy today!

First, I thought I ruined the day! But now Claire says I saved the day!

WE DID IT!!!!

I can't believe that Janice stole Isabel's portfolio. And tried to pretend it was her own. Lauren was pretty mad. She told us we wouldn't be seeing Janice at the premiere tonight.

I hadn't been thinking too much about this ...

I was too upset about losing Isabel's portfolio ...

But now I can just be psyched 'cuz ...

I'm going to be at a movie premiere tonight!

AHHHHHH!!!!

chapter 10

"And then Paulinna said, 'I see some raw talent. It seems you have the drive and the passion, too. Come back to me when you're done with school someday.'"

We were back at the hotel. We were getting ready for the premiere. Claire was curling her hair. Kacey was blow drying her hair. Isabel was painting her nails. And telling us what happened in Paulinna's office.

For the second time. She told us all about it in the cab back. But we wanted to hear it again! Because the story was still so cool even the second time.

"She liked my choice of colors," Isabel was saying. "And she thought my skorts design was very original. Yeeeesss! The great Paulinna said my design was original!"

Isabel was all smiley and glowy!

"That's so wonderful," Claire said. "I feel so proud of you."

"Thanks, Claire," Isabel said. "And thanks again, Maddy. You really came through. First, for talking me into going. And second, for finding my portfolio!"

And Isabel gave me a hug!

Yay!

- Knock! -

Lauren stuck her head in the door.

"Fifteen minute warning! And then we have to go!" she said.

"Yeep!" Kacey squeaked. "My hair's not even dry!"

We all started rushing around to get ready. I took out my outfit.

THE outfit. The Brittany/Movie Star Perfect-for-a-Premiere outfit. I got dressed and looked in the mirror.

"I'm ready," Isabel said. "Anyone want me to do their nails?"

Isabel looked awesome in a black and white striped dress.

"I do!" I said.

I looked through the polishes ...

Cherry Popsicle ... Icy Pink ... Diva Red ...

Usually I'd like Icy Pink! But I'm def more Diva Red in this outfit!

"How about Diva Red?" I asked. "That kinda matches my outfit."

"Sure," Isabel said. "That outfit's different for you. I've never seen you wear anything like that before."

She started painting my nails.

"Yeah," I said. "But I knew this would be perfect for a premiere. Brittany saw it in a magazine. On this actress at a premiere. So I knew I had to get it."

"Do you like it?" Isabel asked.

Do I like it?

I looked down.

"It is a little ... crazy wild for me, I guess," I confessed. "Maybe not exactly my style. But hey I'll just watch Brittany and the movie stars! Tada. That's my new style. I can't screw up."

"Maddy, this is what Paulinna said," Isabel told me. "'Copying other peoples' looks isn't style. You need to find your own style.'"

"Yeah, yeah," I said. "Easy for you to say! You're like this major fashion person. Face it! I have no style! My friend Petie says she has no style! But she doesn't want one so that's cool for her! But I want one!"

"Style is when you're feeling like you're you," Isabel said.

"Well, actually, right now I just feel itchy," I said. This sweater! Seriously itchy! I like my clothes soft. Comfy! Not like a kajillion mosqitos are biting my neck.

I scratched at the fur collar thingy.

"Ready, girls?" Lauren came in.

"And that's the end of Isabel Fashion 101," Isabel said. "For now."

Kacey came out. She was wearing this scooter dress. Super cute! So Kacey! Claire walked out, too. She was wearing a dress that had flowers on it. And a flower pinned by the neck. So pretty! So Claire!

I walked out. Still scratchy.

"OK, we're ready!" Lauren said. "Except ... Maddy?"

Everyone looked at me. And went ... "Oh! Your sweater."

I looked down. There was a red smotchy mess on my sweater! Oh no! From the Diva Red nail polish! I'd been scratching!

I had bright red nail polish all over the top of my sweater!!!

"Oh no!!!! My nails weren't dry!" I said. "I can't go like this!"

"You can borrow something of mine," Claire said. "I'd be happy to lend you an outfit. Want to try something on?"

"Girls, I'm sorry but we just don't have a lot of time," Lauren said. "The car is downstairs. We can't be late!"

"Maddy!" Isabel said. "I have an idea! Put your t-shirt from before back on!"

My t-shirt?

"I can't wear a t-shirt to a movie premiere!!!!" I was like Nooo!

"Hurry!" Kacey was yelling.

So I put it on.

It was one of my favorites. It was white and sparkly with a pink puppy on it. And the puppy was wearing a princess crown.

Isabel ran over with a pink scarf. She tied it around my waist in this funky way.

"Hm ..." She looked me over. "One more thing would tie it together ..."

"How 'bout your hat?" she said.

I put my pink newsboy hat on. I started to take off the pin with Buggie's picture on it.

"Girls! Hurry!" Lauren said.

"Leave the pin," Isabel said. "Come on! Let's go!"

We raced out of the bathroom! We raced to the elevator! And went down through the lobby! And out on the street to a limo!

Whoa! And not just any limo! A big long stretch limo that was ...

Pink?!!!

"The movie studio sent it for you. Fits with the princess theme," Lauren explained.

Ohmigosh!

The driver held the door open for us. We all jumped in the limo. I was in one of the backwards seats. I sat next to Kacey. Claire and Isabel sat across from us.

"Welcome," the driver said. "We will now proceed to the world premiere of *The Princess Movie*! Please help yourself to the beverages and snacks."

"Check this out!" Isabel said. "Everything is pink!"

Pink lemonade! In pink cups!

Pink mints!

Pink napkins!

Princessy Pink!

"Maddy, I like your outfit!" Claire said. "You look really nice."

"Yeah! You look so fun! So puppyish!" Kacey said.

I did feel kinda fun. OK, I was wearing this ordinary t-shirt. But with the scarf, hat, and flippy skirt it looked pretty cool.

"Thanks!" I said.

"Our first stop is the red carpet," Lauren said. "This is how I'd like you to help out. You know how the red carpet works, right?" This is what she told us:

- ☆ The movie stars and other movie people will get out of the limo.
- ☆ They'll walk down the red carpet.
- ☆ They'll stop so the press can take photos and ask questions.
- ☆ Then they'll go in to the movie.

"We're going to put up photos and interviews on a website," Lauren said. "So we need pictures and interviews from the red carpet."

She gave us each a badge on a rope to put around our necks.

"Here's your press pass," she said. "You can stand with the press at the red carpet!"

"So, you will ask the stars questions as they walk by," Lauren said. "You might want to take turns. And get some photos, too."

"We get to talk to the stars?!!" Kacey was almost bouncing through the roof!

COOLNESS!

"Start thinking of questions you'd like to ask the stars," Lauren said. "They move quickly, so just plan one or two questions."

We drove a little bit.

"LOOK!" Kacey yelled. "I see it! I see the theater!"

"We're here a little early," Lauren said. "The street is still blocked off. Pretty soon you'll see all the limos pulling in. And it will get pretty crowded!"

The limo stopped. We were here!

Here at the ...

Movie Premiere!

chapter 11

OK, so this is what the red carpet looked like.

It was ... pink!

No, I'm serious! This red carpet was pink! Lauren told us sometimes the movie people change the carpet color to match the theme. Like, orange or even zebra striped or something! Like green for a green monster movie!

Or pink for a princess movie!

The carpet was roped off on each side. So everyone would stand outside the ropes. And not squish the movie stars.

The limo driver opened the door for us. Kacey got out first and started heading for the theater.

"Hey!" I said. "This is our first red carpet. Shouldn't we do this glamorously?"

"Would you hold my camera for a second?" I asked Lauren. "I'm a fabulous movie star now."

I held up my hand to the limo driver. He took it and helped me out of the car. I started walking down the red carpet.

Kacey, Claire and Isabel all went like this:

"AHHHHHH!!!! It's Maddy Sparks!!!! AHHHHH!"

Like crazy fans!!! I was cracking up!

"Hello, fans!" I said. "Hello, dahlings!"

I waved from the red carpet. I was waving at my fans. I blew kisses at the TOO Crew.

They were like, "AHHHHHH! We love you Maddy!!! We want your autograph!!!"

There were a bunch of people setting up things like lights and stuff. Some photography equipment. They were looking at us like, who are those crazy girls?!!!

I waved to them like I was a movie star.

"Maddy! Over here! Over here!" It was Lauren! She was pretending to take my picture! Hee! Lauren was getting into it, too!

I turned. I gave my best supermodel pose.

CLICK!

Lauren took a real picture of me walking down the red carpet.

"Maddy! Maddy!" Kacey and Isabel were screaming.

I walked down the red carpet. Pretty gracefully.

"Ms. Sparks, TOO Crew Times," Isabel said. "Are you psyched for the movie premiere?"

"Yes, dahling, of course," I said. "Next question."

"Who did your outfit?" Kacey asked me.

"My fabulously talented personal dresser, Isabel Vega chose this for me," I said. "Soon all the celebrities will be wearing her original designs!"

Isabel bowed, thank you, thank you.

"Maddy, is it true you have a secret crush? Who is it on?"

"Ohmigosh!" I said. "What kind of question is that!"

"I'm being a gossip reporter," Kacey explained. "I need a scandal."

"No scandals! No gossip reporting on this red carpet," Lauren was smiling and laughing. "Move along."

"My manager says I have no more time for you paparazzi!" I said, laughing. "Ta ta! Buh-bye!"

I waved to imaginary fans. I blew kisses to the imaginary crowds.

We were all totally cracking up!!!

It was silly! But even PRETENDING to be on that red carpet ...

Way glamorous!

Lauren showed us to an area on the other side of the rope.

"This is where you guys will stand," Lauren said. "You're in the Press Line. The fans are going to be on the other side of the red carpet. The stars will stop by this side for interviews and pictures."

Lauren checked her text messages.

"Let's go check on things inside for a little bit," Lauren said. "Then we'll get you set up out here."

And we went inside the theater.

And we all went, "WOW!"

The theater looked awesome! It was all pink and silver. Like, there were pink and silver lights around the movie screen. There were pink and silver streamers too.

And there were movie posters from the movie everywhere!

Lauren asked us to wait while she checked on some stuff.

"Let's get a game plan for interviewing," Isabel said. "We should take turns for each star."

"That would be fair," Claire agreed.

"We could say we were from the TOO Crew News or something," I said. "Make it official."

"Fun! Let's ask Lauren!" Kacey said. Lauren came over and we asked.

"Sure, no problem. We can call it that on the website!" Lauren said. "We're ready to go outside for red carpet time. They unblocked the street. Everyone's arriving."

We went back outside. And ...

WHOA!

It was CRA-ZAY! There were people EVERYWHERE! Fans on the fan side! People with cameras and stuff on the Press Line! People running around with walkie talkies setting up things.

We went to our special area! We were ready.

I felt kinda nervous!

What if I said something stupid?

What if a movie star came down the line and was like, "Why do I have to talk to that girl?"

What if I knocked something over and it spilled all over some big movie star and they threw me out and it was captured on TV and everyone saw it and ...

"Look!" Kacey screamed. "Here come the limos!!!!"

A huge line of limos was coming! Some of them were pink like the one we came in!

Ohmigosh!

Here come the movie stars!

Everyone was like, "Ahhhhh!"

A couple people came walking down the carpet.

"Don't recognize them ..." Kacey said.

"Maybe people who worked on the movie or something?"

And then the crowd started going like, "EEEEHHHH!"

It was one of the stars!

It's Cadyn Christopher! She plays the sister of the princess! She went over and was signing autographs on the fan side. Then she stopped to get her picture taken. Then she signed more autographs!

That's a seriously busy red carpet!

There was a woman with her. Lauren had told us the stars walked with their publicists to help them out. So nobody tried to keep them too long. Or asked them embarrassing questions and stuff.

Cadyn Christopher was coming our way! She stopped and gave an interview to the people next to us. They had some giant equipment. Like, a giant camera with really bright lights. And a huge microphone.

We had a little microphone. And a digital camera. But we were ready!

"Cadyn! How was the mood on the set?" the reporter asked her.

Cadyn was like, "Great, it was fun!"

And then she came over to us!!! We were up!

Claire was going to interview the first star!

"Hi Cadyn! I really enjoyed your performance on your TV show," Claire said politely.

"Thanks!" Cadyn said. She waited a minute.

"And it's nice meeting you!" Claire said.

"You, too!" Cadyn smiled. "I hope you like the movie!"

And Cadyn moved on!

"No offense, Claire," Isabel said. "But did you forget something?"

"Oh!" Claire said. Her face turned pink. "I forgot to ask my question!"

"Well, you gave her some nice compliments," Isabel said.

And Cadyn was way nice!

Claire was always so nice, too! But it was kinda funny she forgot the question.

Kacey's turn to interview a movie star!

Who would be next?

"I see someone ... I see someone coming ..." Isabel said. "It's Johnny Ray!"

"The TV star?" Kacey said. "I didn't know he was in the movie."

"He's not, actually," Lauren said. "But sometimes stars come to premieres because they're friends with people involved in the movie. Or they're trying to get publicity for something they're working on."

Johnny Ray was coming near us ... closer ... closer ...

"OK! I'm ready!" Kacey said. Here he comes!

CLICK!

I got his picture.

"Johnny! I'm Kacey from TOO Crew News. What are you working on next?" Kacey asked him.

"You'll see me in a TV show this fall," he said to her. "I'll play a guy who's a pro hockey player and a major league baseball player all at once."

"Oh that's so cool!" Kacey said. "That's kinda like me, I play soccer and run track, and softball, but I never played hockey and ..."

Kacey was talking away! Johnny Ray was totally listening but then ...

"Thank you!" his publicist kinda pushed him on.

"Whoops!" Kacey laughed. "I think I talked too much."

Isabel's next!

Who's coming down the carpet next ... who would she interview?

"No way! It's Nina Miles!" Isabel said.

Nina Miles? She was a singer we helped at Toopalooza!

We were all like, "NINA! NINA!"

She came over.

"Do you have a question for Nina?" her publicist asked us.

"Hey!" Nina said. "I know these girls! It's the TOO Crew!"

She reached over the railing. And gave us each a hug!

"What are you doing here?" Isabel asked her.

"I recorded a song on the movie soundtrack!" Nina said. "It's so exciting!"

We were like, "Congratulations, Nina!" She looked so great, too!

CLICK!

I got a picture of Isabel interviewing her. She was asking her who designed her outfit.

"OK, Maddy, I'll take the camera so you can do the next interview!" Isabel said.

OK! Here was someone coming! It was Ellen and Breck, the cutest supercelebrity couple! They were so way cute together! Everyone was like awwww!

"You get to interview two stars at once! Lucky!" Isabel said. They came closer ... closer ...

"Sorry, Ellen and Breck have to move on," the publicist said.

Bummer!

"You'll get the next chance," Claire said.

Someone else was coming ... OK ... OK ...

I heard the crowd all excited! Who was it? Who was coming?!!!

Oh! It was ...

STARLIZE!

YEEESS! I get to interview the star!

"Go, Maddy!" Kacey cheered.

Starlize looked amazing in the silvery dress.

"I saw the original sketch for that dress in Paulinna's office!" Isabel sighed.

Starlize was signing autographs. Then she posed for pictures. Then she signed more autographs. And then she was coming our way and ...

I was up!

"Hi, Starlize," I said. "I'm with the TOO Crew News. How did you like playing a princess?"

"It was like a dream come true," she said. "I got to dress up in ball gowns and the dancing was really fun!"

"Thanks!" I said.

"You're welcome," Starlize said. "Oh! Hey! Is that a dog t-shirt?"

"Oh, yeah," I said. Oh no! The star of the movie noticed I was just wearing a t-shirt!

"I was more dressed up but see I got red nail polish on my other shirt ..." I started to explain. But Starlize kept talking.

"That's such a cute Maltese! Do you like Malteses, too?" Starlize said.

"Um, I love every dog," I told her.

"I have a Maltese!" Starlize said. "Her name's Sushi! She's so cute. I taught her this new trick where she ..."

"Starlize!" her publicist said. "We have to move on!"

Everyone was yelling, "Starlize! Over here! Smile for the camera!"

"Wait, I just want to tell this reporter about Sushi's trick," she said. "When I say 'Sushi, roll,' she rolls over! Isn't that the cutest!"

"Starlize! Sweetheart! We need to head in to the premiere!" her publicist said.

"Oh! I have to go! Bye!" Starlize said.

The TOO Crew was all like ...

"MADDY! Starlize was talking to you!!!"

"She was practically blowing off other people to talk to you!" Kacey was all dancing around!

"Your dog shirt really got her attention!" Isabel said.

Sooooo kewl!!!

"Starlize was so nice! And gorgeous!" I said.

"That will be a great interview for the website," Claire said

"Claire, you're up again," Isabel said.

A bunch of people came down the red carpet, but we didn't recognize anyone. And then ...

"Look, there's Paulinna!" Kacey said.

Yup! Paulinna was walking down the red carpet. All her assistants were around her. And also ...

"And hey ... isn't that Sofia??!" I pointed.

"Sofia? What's my cousin doing on the red carpet?" Isabel asked.

"Sofia! Sofia! Over here!" Kacey shrieked.

Sofia came running over.

"Girls! I'm so excited to tell you this! Paulinna asked me to be a student intern at her office! She said I could start right now ... and here I am! It's a dream come true! Thanks to the TOO Crew!"

We were like, "YAY!!! Yay Sofia!"

And then Paulinna came over.

"Hello again, young ladies," she said.

"Starlize's dress is gorgeous!" Isabel told her, shyly.

"Thank you," Paulinna said. "Someday perhaps you will see your designs on the red carpet as well."

She started to walk away. Then she stopped in front of me.

"Cute puppy," she said, pointing to my hat. "I used to have a darling shih tzu myself."

And then she walked on.

"Sofia got a job with Paulinna! That's so cool!!" I said.

"And that's so cool she noticed your Buggie pin," Kacey said to me.

Isabel didn't say anything! She was all smiling really huge!

Hee!

"And now, it's Claire's turn to interview someone," Isabel reminded us.

"Maybe this time I'll remember to ask a question!" Claire smiled.

The crowd started going crazy ...

Way crazy! Totally out of control! Everyone was like, "CARTER! Over here! CARTER!"

Yes! Here comes ...

CARTER MCLAIN!!!

OK, how much do we luuuuuuuuv him!???! Brownish-blonde hair! Big brown eyes! The way he's so prince looking in the movie poster!

EEEEEEEEEEEEEEEEEEEEEEEEEEEEEE!!!!!!!!!!!!

Carter ran over to the fan line. And he was high-fiving people! Shaking hands! Signing autographs! Giving hugs!

And then he went over to the Press Line! And he was all, "Hi everyone!"

Everyone was like, "CARTER!!!"

And then ... he was coming our way!

"Carter, may I please ask you a question?" Claire asked, politely.

But she was kinda shoved out of the way! By this reporter next to us.

"Carter!!" the reporter was yelling. "Is it true you got in a fistfight on the set with one of your co-stars?" she was asking.

"What?" Carter said. "No way!"

Carter's publicist looked over. "That is simply not true. Next question."

"Carter?" Claire said, in her polite voice. But it was way noisy. He couldn't hear her!

Carter started to walk by ...

And then Claire goes like this ...

"CARTER! OVER HERE!!"

In this major yelly voice!!!!

"Wow!" Isabel said. "I didn't know she could yell! Go, Claire!"

"Um, pretty please?" Claire finished.

And Carter came over!!!!

"Hi, thanks for coming!" he said.

"Carter, would you mind answering a question or two for the TOO Crew News?" Claire asked, politely.

"Go for it," Carter said.

"What's the best part about being an actor?"

"I get to travel and meet lots of people," Carter said.

"What do you like to do for fun?" Claire asked.

"Go to the movies of course, and play basketball and ride dirt bikes," he answered.

"Thank you for your time, Carter," Claire said.

"Carter! Carter!" people were yelling.

Carter waved bye and had to go!

Bye Carter! Byeeeee!

I looked at Kacey and Isabel and Claire and we all were like ...

"EEEEEEEEEEEEEEEEEEEEEEEE! CARTER MCLAIN!!!!"

"Good job," Isabel told Claire. "You even asked TWO questions."

And then ... OK! People were packing up their stuff. Time to go!

The red carpet was over!

But the movie premiere ... was about to begin!!!!

We started heading inside with the crowd.

"I can't wait to see this movie!" I said. "And see the movie stars!"

"Speaking of movie stars ... why are movie stars so cool?" Kacey asked. "They have so many fans! Get it? Like fans that cool you off?"

And we all yelled ...

"MWAH-HA-HA!"

We made it into the lobby.

"Look! Snacks!" Kacey said. Kacey is seriously snacky! She has like snack radar or something. We went over and stood in line.

"What do dogs eat in the movie theater?" Kacey asked us. "Pupcorn!"

We all were like, "Groan!!!"

"Would you like a Princess Snack Pack?" the person at the counter asked. "It comes with popcorn, lemonade and a choice of candy."

"Ohmigosh, this popcorn is pink!" I said. Then we picked out candies.

I picked pink gummies!

Kacey picked a pink lollipop!

Isabel picked pink and white peppermints!

And Claire picked pink jellybeans!

And we all got pink lemonade to drink.

"Time to go inside, girls," Lauren said. She gave us each a ticket to find our seat.

The movie theater was full of people. It was kinda dark.

We saw the winners up front. In the seats with the crowns we'd decorated.

"Guess who also gets to sit near the front?" Lauren asked.

The TOO Crew!!

"I'll check on our contest winners and join you in a minute," Lauren said.

We were near the front row. But kinda way in the middle. So we had to walk past some people already sitting in the row. I followed Isabel, Claire and Kacey in. They got to our seats.

"Excuse me!" I said. It was tricky. Carrying the camera bag. Carrying my snack pack. Trying not to bump anyone.

We were all like, "Excuse me! Excuse me!"

And then ... I stepped on this guy's foot.

Uh oh! I was losing my balance! I was slipping! I was falling ... I grabbed my drink so it wouldn't spill! But ...

ACK! I fell!!!!!!

And the popcorn flew everywhere!

Landing right on the guy!

And I did, too!

I FELL RIGHT INTO THE GUY'S LAP!

Oh no!

"Sorry, sorry!" I was saying. Then I looked at the guy and ...

OH.

MY.

GOSH.

The guy was ...

CARTER MCLAIN!

Red-face Rating: ☆★★ out of ☆★★★☆ stars.
ACK! But at least it's kinda dark in here.

Then FLASH! There was a flash of light! And a ...

CLICK!

Make that ...

Red-face Rating: ☆★★★★ out of ☆★★★★☆ stars.
I think one of the reporters just took a picture!

chapter 12

OhmigoshOhmigoshOhmigosh!

"Well, hello," Carter said.

I jumped up. OK! I gotta get outta here!

"Who took that picture?" the woman next to him was yelling, turning around. "You! With the camera! As Carter McLain's publicist I demand you give me that film!"

She pushed past me. And knocked me right over again.

"Ohmigosh, I'm SO sorry," I said. Carter McLain was covered in popcorn. PINK popcorn. MY pink popcorn.

"I'm fine," Carter said. "You did me a favor. I don't really like this shirt they picked out for me today, anyway. Now I don't have to wear it again."

"Maddy! You OK?" Isabel was coming over.

Then Carter goes.

"You look familiar. Don't I know you?"

"You sang to her at a party!" Isabel told him.

"Hey! I remember. You're the frog slippers girl!"

Um, yes! I was! Because see last time I saw him I was wearing these giant frog slippers and ...

He remembered!!!!

"So how ya doin?" Carter was saying. "Have a seat til my publicist gets back."

He patted at the seat next to him.

Uh ...

"GLAK!"

OK! Well, what would YOU say if #2 on YOUR Ultimate Crush List who is also a famous movie star asked you that?!!!

I sat.

Next to Carter McLain!

"I remember those frog slippers," Carter was saying. As he was brushing popcorn kernels off himself. "They reminded me of when I lived back home. Growing up we went frogging all the time and ..."

I just sat there. Like ... GAH!!!!

And then Carter's publicist came back! I got up so she could have her seat.

I hope she got that film back. At least she could get rid of the evidence of my fall.

"Carter darling, I let that photographer keep the film. He convinced me you'd look like a hero, saving a falling girl. And also he'd land you a cover on his magazine next month."

Carter was like, "OK, sure, fine."

But I was like ... wait a minute. They won't print a picture of me falling on Carter McLain ... will they?

"Maddy, we should probably sit down," Isabel whispered.

"OK, bye!" I said. "Sorry again!" Carter said bye and Isabel and I went over to our seats.

I didn't fall on anybody else.

Whew.

I sat down next to Kacey.

"EEEE!"

Kacey and Claire were all like, "Maddy fell on Carter McLain!"

I looked over. Lauren was talking to the Carter McLain people, making sure they were OK I guess.

"OK, Most Embarrassing Moment ever," I said. "I can't believe I did that."

"I got you replacement snacks," Lauren handed me a new Princess Snack Pack.

"Thanks, Lauren!"

"Carter says to tell you it was nice to see you again, Frog Slippers," Lauren said. "Those were his words exactly."

I couldn't help smiling. I was feeling way better now.

Yum! I leaned back in my squishy chair. I popped some popcorn in my mouth. I ripped open the bag of pink gummies.

Ahhhh ... life is good.

And then ...

The lights went dark and ...

The screen went bright and ...

The movie was on!!!

OK ... how cool is this?

I get to watch a movie ...

At the world premiere ...

I can see the stars of the movie sitting near me ...

With my friends next to me!

The music started! The credits started rolling on the screen!

Starring Starlize.

The crowd jumped up! Standing ovation! I jumped up too! We were all like, "WOOHOO!" Clap clap clap! "Yay Starlize!"

And then on the screen it said ...

And starring ... Carter McLain as the Prince!

The crowd was like "WOOOHOOO!!! CARTER!!!!" Clap clap clap! We were all going crazy!

Carter stood up! He turned around and waved to the audience.

"Just think, Maddy," Claire sighed. "That's your popcorn

sticking all over his shirt."

 !!!!!!!!!!

chapter 13

We were on the plane home. I was sitting with the TOO Crew. I looked across the aisle. Lauren was reading a magazine, my Dad was on his laptop. Bruno was snoozing.

Kacey was at the window seat. I leaned over her and watched out the window as the plane went up ... up ... up!

I watched the plane circle over the skyscrapers.

"Look! There's the Empire State Building!" Kacey said.

"I can't believe we went to the top of it," I said.

"I think I see Central Park," Claire said.

"OK, how funny was that when we were running with the marathon racers. Like, we must get to Isabel! We must save her portfolio!" Kacey cracked up.

"I heard someone who thought Maddy was winning the race!" Claire laughed.

"You guys were my heroes," Isabel said. "And I still can't believe Paulinna liked my designs!"

"So cool," I agreed.

"There's the Statue of Liberty," Claire pointed.

New York City got smaller and smaller ... and then we were up through the clouds.

Bye, New York City!

I settled back in my seat.

"What do you get if you cross a dog with an airplane?" Kacey asked. "A jet setter! Mwah-ha-ha."

"Weak," I laughed.

"That trip was really fun," Claire said.

"That movie was soooo good," I said. "Two thumbs up! Five out of five stars! A must-see!"

"Loved the wardrobe," Isabel said.

"Carter McLain was sooooo cute," Claire said. "When he looked into Starlize's eyes and was like, 'You are my princess ...'"

We were all like ... "EEEEEEEEEEEEEE!"

Soooo romantic!

"It was just how he looked when he looked into Maddy's eyes ... when she fell on him in the movie theater," Isabel teased.

"Hey!" I swopped her arm.

"Don't mess with Maddy," Kacey warned. "She'll spill popcorn on you!"

"So tell us again what Carter said to you!" Claire said to me.

"First, he said 'ouch,'" I remembered. Yeeps. I did step on his foot pretty hard.

"Then he remembered Maddy from the sleepover party!" Isabel said. "Seriously, how cool is it that he recognized her!"

Yeah, OK! That part was way cool!

"It must have been the frog slippers," Claire said. "Wearing huge googly frog slippers with a ball gown is pretty memorable."

"Carter also said he was glad I ruined his shirt because someone else picked it out for him. And it wasn't his style," I told them.

The plane was getting kinda warm. I took off my sweatshirt.

"Cute," Claire said, pointing at my shirt with the puppy and kitten snuggling on it.

"This shirt reminds me of my little Buggie," I said. "I can't wait to see her!"

"Maddy!" Isabel said. "Guess what! I just realized something."

"Um, what?"

"You've figured out YOUR style on this trip!!!!" Isabel said.

OK, huh?

"My style is a tripping, klutzy popcorn spiller?" I asked.

"No! Get this! Style is about wearing stuff that is really YOU, right?" Isabel said.

"Oook ...? I'm still not getting it ..."

"OK, you wore frog slippers you liked, right?" Isabel said. "Your puppy shirts, your kitten shirt, even your Buggie pin on the hat ..."

"OK ..."

"So your style is Animal Lover!" Isabel said.

Ohhhhhhhhhhhhh! I get it!

"It's so you!" Isabel said. "You're always so happy in your

style. And also, it's a great conversation starter. Like when you wore those frog slippers? Carter was like, I like frogs too!"

"Yeah!" Kacey said. "And your puppy shirt made Starlize stop and talk to you about dogs! And even Paulinna talked about dogs 'cuz of your Buggie pin!"

"When you're in your style, everyone knows what to talk about to you!" Isabel said.

"Even famous movie stars!" Claire added.

Yeah! That's all pretty true!

So hey ....

I have a style!

Kewl!!!

Me! My own style!

"Excuse me, girls?" my Dad said. He was sitting across the aisle from us. "Something about your movie premiere just came up on entertainment news online."

He passed his laptop over to me. Everyone leaned in to see.

It was a news website. The headline read:

ENTERTAINMENT NEWS:
The Princess Movie Premieres

Tween superstars Starlize and Carter McLain were on hand to promote their new movie at the worldwide premiere.

"Yay! And we were there, too!" Kacey said.

"Look, you can click to see photos," Isabel suggested.

I clicked.

It was a picture of Starlize in her silvery gown and tiara. She looked beautiful!

Next! A picture of cutest couple Ellen and Breck. Awwww!

Next! A picture of Carter and Starlize! Awwww!

Next! A picture that said EXCLUSIVE!

It was of Carter with a girl falling over him! Awww ...

Hey ...

Wait one second ...

Not, awwwww ...

ACK!!!!!

I looked closer. Was it? Was it?

"MADDY!" Kacey, Isabel, and Claire were screaming. "It's YOU! It's YOU!"

Yeek! It was that picture of me! Yes. It was true. There I was. Falling over. Popcorn spilling. On the website for everyone to see.

"The caption says ..." Isabel started to read. "Teen heartthrob Carter McLain has girls falling all over him at the movie premiere."

"Ohmigosh," I said. "This is way embarrassing."

Everyone was trying not to laugh ...

Kacey was turning red.

Isabel was biting her lip.

Claire was hiding her face in her hands.

OK. It WAS pretty funny.

I couldn't help it. I busted out laughing.

And everyone LOST IT! Totally cracking up!

"Girls are falling all over him!" Claire was gasping for breath. "That's so funny."

We couldn't stop laughing.

Ohmigosh! Ohmigosh! We were all flopped over the airline seats. Laughing so hard. People were like, those girls are crazy!!!

"Can't breathe," Kacey said. "Too funny."

We finally calmed down. Whew!

"Maddy, there was also an e-mail waiting for you," my Dad said. "From one of your friends? Brittany? It said you should go to this website?"

Huh? I clicked on the link.

I saw loading ... hair ... heads ... faces ... oh!

"It's my class picture!" I said. "They posted it online."

Kacey looked over my shoulder.

Isabel leaned across my arm.

Claire leaned over the seat.

There I was. In my jeans. In my white shirt.

Kacey was turning red. "Um, your smile looks way great!" she said.

Claire was hiding her face in her hands. "And your hair looks nice."

Isabel was biting her lip. "And your white shirt is, uh, crisply ironed."

But OK, everyone was trying not to laugh.

Because ... MY EYES WERE CLOSED!

"You blinked!" they all yelled.

"Oh noooo!" I wailed. "I look like I'm asleep or something!"

And then I stopped.

"Well, at least nobody will notice my outfit."

And then I couldn't help it. I busted out laughing. And we were all ...

TOTALLY CRACKING UP!

And then Isabel says, "Wait, check out Brittany."

"Yeah, yeah," I sighed. "I know. Her outfit is way cool, right?"

"No, look," Isabel said. "Zoom in on that teeny little square there."

I zoomed. I zoomed in closer.

"Wait a minute," Kacey said. "Is that a ... tag?"

Oh. My. Gosh!!!!!!

"Brittany's shirt ... is on backwards!" we all screamed.

"Looks like Brittany's last minute change was a little too rushed," Isabel said.

"She e-mailed this to everyone. She must not have noticed!" I said.

"Yet, anyway," Kacey said.

Hee.

(But next year ... I'm going to wear a shirt with a dog on it!!!!)

"OK, here's a joke," Isabel said.

"Oh no!" I groaned. "Not you, too, with the jokes!"

"Knock, knock," said Isabel.

"Who's there?" we all answered.

"Frank," Isabel said.

"Frank who?"

"Frank you for being my friends!" Isabel said. "The TOO Crew ROCKS!!!!!"

And we all yelled out ...

"MWAH-HA-HA!!!!"

Happy Face Rating:

 out of

The end ...

OK but you know it's not REALLY the end. 'Cuz more good stuff's going to happen! You've just gotta get TUNED IN!

the **too crew's**
stuff for you to do

My Movie Madness!

Fave movie: _____

Fave movie star: _____

Last movie I saw was: _____

My fave kind of movie is:

- ☐ Funny one
- ☐ Sweet one
- ☐ Scary one
- ☐ Adventure one

If a movie star were going to play me in a movie, it would be:

_____

name of movie star

My BFF would be played by what movie star:

_____

name of movie star

If I were walking down a red carpet, I would wear:

_____

_____

_____

_____

_____

_____

If I were a movie star, this would be my autograph for my fans: (sign your name in the space below!)

This Journal Belongs to:

Maddy Elizabeth Sparks

OK! You guys! I gotta go! It's over! But not forever of course!

Because I'll be back. With Kacey! And Isabel! And Claire!

I mean, we have more glam trips to take! More TOO Crew stuff to do!

Like in Episode #9! Coming exclusively to Limited Too!!!!

Luv ya! ♡

♡

Maddy

♡

PS Hey! Did you check out LimitedToo.com???!!!!

'Cuz the TOO Crew has this totally brand new section on it. Yes! A section about Tuned In!

I'm way serious!

And it's got a sneak preview of Episode #9! And more stuff on it! Some INSIDE SCOOP!

Go check it out! Because you're not going to believe what happens next!

www.limitedtoo.com